A sister's untold journey brought to life like never before!



# GRETE'S METAMORPHOSIS

## A Retelling of Franz Kafka's Timeless Tale

Ram Khatri

*Illustrated by Sandipan Santra*

**E-mail:** publishing@ramckhatri.com

**Author website:** www.ramckhatri.com

This novella is an experimental adaptation of *The Metamorphosis*, reimagining Kafka's story from a new perspective. While keeping Kafka's characters and world, it serves as an independent exploration of literature through artificial intelligence.


Published by
Restart Publishing, LLC

FIRST EDITION, 2025

**ISBN:** 978-1-7377552-7-2 (Paperback)
**ISBN:** 978-1-7377552-8-9 (eBook)

A reimagined adaptation by **Ram Khatri**, powered by **AI**

Illustrations by
**Sandipan Santra**

Cover Design: **REBECACOVERS**

Design & Production: **Inshrah Tariq**

www.facebook.com/books.ramckhatri

www.instagram.com/ramchandrak

This novella is an experimental adaptation of *The Metamorphosis,* reimagining Franz Kafka's story from a new perspective. While keeping Kafka's characters and world, it serves as an independent exploration of literature through artificial intelligence.

# FOREWORD

The first time I read *The Metamorphosis*, I was a literature student in Kirtipur, a university town in Nepal. Its opening line struck me like a sudden gust of wind—unsettling, yet strangely familiar. I devoured the novella in one sitting, then wandered to a small restaurant, where I ordered a cup of milk tea and began to ponder with every sip.

That day, something felt different. A thought lingered in my mind like a persistent shadow: *What if I woke up blind tomorrow?* The fear settled deep within me, refusing to let go. It was 2003, and I had just started wearing glasses prescribed by my doctor.

Kafka's story unsettled me in ways I couldn't yet name, but it never left me. Over the years, it resurfaced like an old melody, whispering its weight into my thoughts. It pushed me to translate *The Metamorphosis* into Nepali. And now, it has led me here—to this adaptation that invites you to step into Grete's world.

We often remember Grete as Gregor's devoted sister, but have we ever stopped to wonder about her metamorphosis? Caught between love and exhaustion, duty and self-preservation, she, too, transforms—only more quietly. Her journey forces us to ask: *When does care turn into sacrifice? When does love demand a price?*

This adaptation also embraces storytelling's evolving nature. I explore the delicate dance between human imagination and machine assistance by weaving artificial intelligence into the creative process.

So, I invite you to step closer and look again. *Who truly undergoes the greater metamorphosis—Gregor or Grete?*

**Ram Khatri**

**March 2025**

# CONTENTS

# 1

## The Door Between Us

I n our house, silence is the loudest thing of all. It presses down on us like a crushing weight, suffocating every moment. I am Grete Samsa, seventeen years old, and my family's silence is as thick and unyielding as a fog that won't lift. We speak. We move. Yet, we are mere marionettes, our strings pulled by unseen hands, our lives unfolding in perfect, suffocating harmony. A fragile thread tethers my father, mother, and brother Gregor, and that thread is Gregor himself.

Gregor, my older brother, is twenty-four. He is our reluctant savior, a traveling salesman whose weary feet have borne the weight of our family for years. Since Father's business collapsed, leaving us buried in debt and struggling to make ends meet, Gregor has been the only source of hope we cling to. He leaves before dawn, the sound of his shoes on the wooden floor like a steady drumbeat, marking the beginning of yet another day spent trudging through the grind. His briefcase holds more than just sample goods; it is the lifeline of our survival, the hope that one day we might find ourselves whole again. And when he returns, he is a little more worn and quieter each evening. His silence speaks louder than words could, echoing with sacrifices too heavy to articulate.

Then there's my father, who once commanded respect with his words, now reduced to a slouched figure. He spends his days flipping through newspapers, searching for a past that has slipped beyond his grasp. His eyes are hollow, his gaze distant, as if waiting for something—perhaps for the world to right itself or Gregor to keep fixing it for him. His past, a shadow of his former self, haunts the present. My mother, too, is a ghost of herself, fluttering through the house like a tired bird, her frail fingers, once nimble with the threads of creation, now fumbled with the simplest tasks, each movement a testament to the weight she carried. And me? I'm a girl caught between childhood and adulthood, watching a world I once thought full of possibilities slip through my fingers like water.

But everything changed that morning. The morning, Gregor didn't open his door. His absence was like a gaping hole in the fabric of our lives, a void that threatened to swallow us whole.

It was an ordinary winter day where frost clings to the windowpanes like stubborn memories, and the air inside feels colder than it should. The light outside was pale, struggling against the weight of the heavy curtains that shielded us from the world. I was stitching ribbons into hats, trying to focus on the delicate task. Each pull of the needle felt like a small victory, a brief escape from the worries that piled up in my mind. But then, as if on cue, Mother's voice shattered the fragile quiet, disrupting our daily routine and adding to the tension in the house.

"Gregor! You'll miss your train!" Her words were sharp, trembling. She knocked softly at first, then louder, the sound growing more insistent. There was a desperation in her voice, a crack in the perfect façade we all wore that I had never heard before.

I heard her slippers shuffle from the hallway, each step heavier than the last. I had grown used to this sound, which usually signified nothing more than her habitual movements. But today, it felt different. Each step seemed to reverberate through the house, vibrating through the walls as if it were holding its breath.

I paused, my fingers stilling on the ribbon. A cold shiver slid down my spine. Something was wrong.

"What's he doing in there?" Mother's voice was brittle now, each word a thin thread pulled taut. Her voice, usually soft and controlled, now cracked at the edges. Each knock echoed through the house, like the sound of breaking glass.

Sitting in his armchair and rustling the newspaper as always, Father lowered it just enough to peer over the top. His eyes were dark with impatience, a storm brewing beneath the surface.

"That boy knows what's at stake. He wouldn't dare mess this up." His words were a sharp reminder of the precarious balance we were all teetering on.

What's at stake? The words lingered, heavy and accusing. Gregor was not just our breadwinner; he was our lifeline. Without him, we were nothing. The thought of losing him—whether to illness, failure, or something else entirely—was unthinkable. But the silence in the room seemed to whisper otherwise. The fear of losing Gregor was a constant, looming presence, making the family feel vulnerable and exposed.

"Grete, go talk to him," Mother urged, her voice small and fragile, a plea for help in a situation she couldn't control. She looked at me with desperate eyes, her silent plea hanging between us. "He'll listen to you." Her hope was a fragile thread, barely holding against the weight of the impending crisis. The desperation in her voice was palpable, a reflection of the family's dire need for Gregor's cooperation.

Would he? The thought felt more like a question than an answer. Gregor and I had once been close, sharing secrets and dreams of a future that felt real. But now, there was nothing but distance between us, a chasm filled with silence and unspoken resentments.

I stood, hesitated for a moment, and then made my way to his door. Each step echoed in the hallway, each one heavier than the last. My hand hovered over the doorknob, its calm surface sending a ripple of unease through me. I knocked softly. "Gregor?" I called, my voice barely more than a whisper. There was no response—just the faintest sound, like the brush of fabric against the floor.

"Maybe he's just overslept," I offered, though I knew they weren't true even as the words left my mouth. Gregor never overslept.

Father, his patience worn thin, rose with a growl. Each step toward the door was deliberate, his heavy footsteps echoing like distant thunder, a storm on the brink of breaking. He pounded on the door, the force of his fist causing the wood to groan in protest. "Open up, Gregor!" he bellowed. "You hear me?" His voice was not just angry but desperate, a father's plea for his son to be safe.

The house seemed to shudder with the force of his anger. Mother's hands clenched around the banister, her knuckles white. "What if he's ill?" she whispered, her words breaking the tension, a question we all feared to ask.

Father's scowl deepened. "Ill? He can't afford to be ill. None of us can." His words were sharp, each aimed at the heart of our family's fragile existence. But beneath the anger, there was fear—a fear for his son's health, a fear for the family's future, and a fear of his helplessness in the face of this crisis.

I pressed my ear against the door, straining to hear anything—anything that would tell me that Gregor was still the brother I once knew. "Gregor," I called, my voice quivering. "Please, say something. Let us know you're all right."

And then, a faint groan. Barely audible but unmistakable. Relief washed over me, quickly replaced by a new kind of unease. Gregor was alive, but something was terribly wrong.

The hours dragged on, each feeling like a slow, torturous crawl. Mother fluttered nervously from room to room, her worry consuming every movement. Father paced—his frustration was a constant storm that was impossible to stop. And I—well, I stood in the hallway, caught between my childhood and whatever was coming next, unable to focus on anything but that closed door.

By evening, the tension had reached its boiling point. Father's anger spilled over. "He thinks he can just ignore us?" His voice was harsh, his words cutting through the silence like knives. "After everything we've done for him?"

Mother's hands twisted the fabric of her apron. "He's not ignoring us," she whispered. "He's carried us for years. Maybe he's just... tired."

Father's fist slammed onto the table, making the dishes rattle in protest. "Tired? We're all tired. But we don't lock ourselves away, do we?"

His words were cruel but contained a bitter truth we couldn't ignore. Gregor had given so much—his time, energy, and life—so we might survive. And now, it seemed, he had nothing left to give.

That night, I stood outside his door again, my forehead pressed against the cool wood. Memories of happier times—when Gregor and I would laugh and talk when he would play with me—felt like distant fragments. Where had that brother gone? And why did I think so complicit in his disappearance?

Sleep came fitfully, interrupted by strange dreams—whispers I couldn't understand, shadows shifting in the corners of my mind. I dreamt of Gregor, but he was always just out of reach, his face obscured by darkness. When I awoke, the house was still, the silence almost suffocating. Gregor's door remained shut, an impenetrable barrier between us.

But as I stood there, I noticed something that made my heart skip: a faint, almost imperceptible crack in the door, as though it had been pushed open and quickly closed again.

I reached out instinctively, my hand hovering above the doorknob, but then—a sound—a low, muffled groan from inside. My blood ran cold.

Something was terribly wrong. And I knew, deep down, that whatever awaited behind that door would change everything.

# 2

## The Quiet Before the Storm

The morning drifted by, a haze of restless energy that hung over the house like a storm waiting to break. The rhythm that once governed our home—predictable, silent, unnervingly still—had shattered. In its place was an unsettling quiet, a vacuum that swallowed everything it touched. Mother—pale and etched with worry—wandered through the rooms, her hands clutching a handkerchief that trembled in her grip. Each step she took seemed less purposeful than the last, as though she were walking through the ruins of a life she could no longer understand. Her lips moved in a quiet prayer, but her eyes held no faith—only a vast emptiness that mirrored the silence around us. The mother I once knew was slipping away, piece by piece.

Father, by contrast, was a fortress of coldness. He sat in his armchair, rigid and unmoving, arms crossed across his chest and his gaze fixed unflinchingly on the closed door to Gregor's room. Father radiated disapproval, a heavy, suffocating presence filling every corner of the house. The silence between us thickened as he sat there, his eyes boring into the door with such intensity it was as if he could pull Gregor out of hiding. But Gregor didn't answer. Like an invisible force, Father's wrath was so palpable it almost seemed to shift the air, pressing down on us all. The house had become a battlefield, the lines drawn not in visible blood but in the fragile spaces between our unspoken words.

And me? I was suspended in that same fractured space, neither fully a child nor yet an adult. Caught between the expectations of both, I could feel the weight of every glance, every moment of tension, tightening around my chest like an iron chain. I was expected to hold us together, but it felt as though the thread connecting us was fraying with every passing second. The burden of being the unspoken glue was too heavy today, more than it had ever been before.

By mid-morning, I could no longer ignore the pull of Gregor's door. The unanswered questions gnawed at me, turning each moment into a slow, relentless ache. What had happened to him? Why wouldn't he come out? What had shattered the quiet promise of his routine? My body moved toward the door almost against my will, my hands trembling as I carried the tray of weak broth. The smell of overcooked onions clung to the air, trying to fill the hollow spaces of the house with something resembling comfort, but it failed to mask the tension. I knew Gregor wouldn't touch it. The tray offered more than a meal—a feeble attempt at proving that someone still cared and saw him.

"Gregor," I called softly, my voice barely more than a whisper as I approached his door. I paused, my breath hitching in my chest. Knocking felt too intrusive—demanding something that couldn't be forced. "I'm leaving some food here for you," I murmured, as though the simple act could restore normalcy, even for a moment.

I set the tray down gently, careful not to make a sound, then stepped back, my breath shallow in the stillness. I waited, heart pounding, for any sign of life from beyond the door—a footstep, a murmur, a sound of any kind—but nothing. The silence was unbearable until my hope withered into the space.

Turning away, I couldn't help but feel the weight of something far more profound than just disappointment. What had I expected? Would Gregor open the door and reassure us, telling us it was just a mistake or miscommunication and that everything would return to how it had been? As I now knew, the truth was far more complex, lodged in the closed door like a jagged shard, impossible to ignore.

The mirror caught my reflection as I walked down the hallway. I paused, staring at the face that stared back at me. The girl in the glass was a stranger—pale, worn, and haunted. Strands of hair had escaped my braid, and the shadows under my eyes told a story I couldn't escape. I had changed. I wasn't the girl who laughed with Gregor, who dreamed of a different life. Now, I was someone whose days bled into one another, defined by the hollow weight of responsibilities I never asked for but dutifully carried. My heart ached with a mixture of fear, guilt, and a growing sense of helplessness.

For weeks, a foreign feeling had settled within me, a storm I had mistaken for resentment—resentment toward Father's endless frustration, Mother's helplessness, and Gregor for his retreat into silence. But as I stared into my tired eyes, I realized it wasn't resentment. It was exhaustion, a bone-deep weariness that no amount of rest could alleviate. I was tired of carrying this family on my shoulders, of holding our fragile semblance of normality together when all of us were slowly disintegrating. Yet, my sense of duty, my obligation to keep us afloat, was a burden I couldn't shake.

I shook off the thought, forcing my feet to move. The kitchen needed tending—dishes to scrub, laundry to fold, floors to sweep. The routine was my lifeline, the only constant in a sea of chaos threatening to drown us. But even as I worked, my mind wandered, slipping through the cracks of our shattered household.

And then I saw him again.

The boy.

He had become a fixture in my life over the past weeks, passing by our house simultaneously every day. His steps were deliberate and careful, as though he carried some burden too heavy to share. He couldn't have been much older than me—eighteen, maybe nineteen—with dark, unruly hair and eyes that held a quiet kindness I couldn't quite place. Something in his gaze seemed to see more than what was obvious. I couldn't help but watch him as he passed. Once, I had caught him glancing up at the window, his eyes lingering for a moment before he moved on, but I had told myself it was nothing—just a fleeting look, nothing more.

But today, as he walked by, he paused. His eyes flickered up toward the second-floor window—the one that led to Gregor's room. His steps faltered, and his gaze lingered a moment longer. My heart skipped a beat. Could he sense the weight in our house? Could he see the cracks in the façade we had so carefully constructed?

I ducked behind the curtain, heat rising to my cheeks. It wasn't brilliant to even think it mattered. He was just a boy—someone outside our world. But for a brief moment, I allowed myself to imagine a life beyond the walls of this house, a life where someone saw me for more than my duties. It was a dangerous thought that would lead only to disappointment, but one I couldn't help but entertain in my longing for a different life. I could be seen as more than just a caretaker in this life.

By evening, the tension had become unbearable. The tray of broth remained untouched, a silent rejection that dug into my chest like a splinter. Father's anger boiled over at supper, his words sharp and demanding: "Grete, you're the only one he listens to. Do something." I felt the frustration bubbling within me, frustration at our situation, Gregor's silence, and the weight of the expectations placed on me.

"I've tried," I whispered, my voice almost too quiet to be heard. "Gregor won't answer."

"Then try harder," Father snapped, his voice hard, cold. "We can't afford this nonsense. He needs to pull his weight."

Mother's soft voice, always the counterbalance to Father's anger, cut through the tension. "Leave her be," she murmured, her eyes downcast. "She's doing her best."

Father grumbled, but his rage subsided. The silence that followed was thick with blame, unspoken yet undeniable. After dinner, I retreated to my room, the walls closing around me. My eyes drifted to the violin in the corner, its presence a faint reminder of who I used to be.

I picked it up, hesitantly running my fingers across the strings. A single note rang out—haunting, fragile, beautiful. For a fleeting moment, the weight of the day lifted. But as the note faded, reality returned, heavier than before.

Somewhere behind that locked door, Gregor remained silent. And outside, the boy walked on, his footsteps fading into the night.

# 3

## The Weight
## of Silence

The violin rested untouched at the edge of my bed, gleaming in the dim light like an unspoken promise I no longer knew how to keep. It called to me, but I was afraid to respond.

I couldn't bring myself to touch it—not with Gregor's door locked and the air in this house so thick with dread it felt like breathing through the wool. The violin would have to wait. I had too much to do—yet nothing that could change anything. Instead, I threw myself into tasks with frantic energy, scrubbing floors, polishing windows, and ironing linens. Every corner of the house gleamed under my hands. But no amount of work could hide the cracks beneath. The house looked perfect, but it was an illusion. It was a fragile veneer masking something

broken, something no scrubbing could fix.

Dust was everywhere—not just on the furniture, but in the air, settling into the fabric of our lives. It clung to our words, our silences, our every movement. We no longer spoke much. We didn't need to. The house spoke for us; the dust silently witnessed the unraveling that had begun long ago. The harder I worked, the more I felt the weight of the despair that had settled over us. It was like an unwelcome guest, lingering, refusing to leave.

By midday, the whispers began again. They were sharp, cutting through the silence like tiny needles. The housemaid passed me in the hallway, her voice low, her eyes darting nervously toward the stairs. "That thing in the room," she muttered under her breath. A cold knot twisted in my stomach. That thing? Gregor wasn't a thing. He was my brother, no matter what had happened. But now, he was the thing we feared. And in that moment, I hated myself for not knowing how to stop it.

I fought the urge to snap at her, to remind her of who Gregor had been before all of this. But I didn't. I was tired of fighting. We were all tired.

The boy, a neighbor's son, passed the house again that afternoon, as he always did. I saw him through the kitchen window, my knife moving through the potatoes mechanically. His footsteps were slower today, unsure, as though weighed down by something invisible. As he passed, he lingered longer than usual, his gaze locked on the second-floor window that led to Gregor's room. I felt a strange pang in my chest. Was he seeing what we all tried so hard to hide? Could he feel the weight of the silence, the burden we carried, or was it just my imagination?

For a fleeting moment, I envisioned him knocking on the door, stepping inside, and shattering the enchantment that had frozen us all in place. But he didn't. He continued, his shoulders hunched under a weight I couldn't define. As he vanished down the street, my hope dissipated with him. There was nothing he could do. Nothing any of us could do. The boy wasn't a savior. But he was a beacon of hope, a reminder that even in our darkest moments, there was still a glimmer of light.

I set the knife down, watching the half-peeled potato roll across the table. The boy wasn't my savior. I wasn't some tragic figure waiting for someone to come and rescue me. I was Grete Samsa—a girl with calloused hands, a family slowly unraveling, and a silence that choked us all. My life wasn't a story waiting for a hero. It was a burden I had to carry alone.

As the evening stretched into the night and the house settled into its familiar quiet, I picked up my violin again. It wasn't a decision I made. It was as though the violin itself had called me back. My fingers trembled as they gripped the bow, and when I placed the instrument under my chin, it felt like an old friend, one I had neglected for far too long. The first note faltered. It sounded like an apology. But as I played, the music began to flow more freely, filling the room and wrapping around me like a blanket.

Music had always been my sanctuary, where I could articulate the words I couldn't utter. It had once been my voice. But tonight, the music felt different. Each note was a declaration of defiance, a push against the silence engulfing our lives. The music grew stronger and louder each moment until the room seemed to pulse. For a few precious moments, the house felt alive again, the shadows momentarily pushed back by the melody that filled the air, wrapping me in its comforting embrace.

And then, I heard it.

A sound. Faint, almost imperceptible, but unmistakable.

The violin's notes faltered as I strained to listen. A rustling noise came from behind Gregor's door, like fabric brushing against the floor. My heart leaped in my chest, a strange mixture of hope and fear building within me. Was he—was he still there?

"Gregor?" I whispered, almost afraid that speaking his name out loud would break the fragile moment. I set the violin down carefully, trying not to disturb the silence. My feet moved cautiously toward his door, each step an intrusion into the stillness. The floorboards creaked beneath me, an unwelcome sound in the heavy silence.

No response. But the rustling came again, more deliberate this time, followed by a soft, guttural groan—a sound that sent a chill down my spine. I pressed my ear to the door, my breath shallow, waiting for some sign that Gregor was still with us.

"Please," I whispered, my voice a faint plea. "Say something. Let me help you."

The silence was more profound than before as if the house had stopped breathing. I leaned closer, desperate for any sign, any sound that would tell me he was still there. But there was nothing—just the pounding of my heart echoing in my ears.

"Grete, leave him be," my mother's voice came from behind me, startling me out of my thoughts. She stood in the dim hallway, her frail figure barely visible. Her voice was soft but firm, a quiet command wrapped in fear. "He needs time. That's all."

I wanted to argue, to tell her that time was no longer enough, that something was wrong. But the look in her eyes stopped me. It was the look of someone who had surrendered and accepted that no one could do anything. She was as helpless as I was. As powerless as we all were.

Reluctantly, I stepped back. "Come downstairs," my mother said, her voice trembling. "There's nothing more you can do tonight."

I followed her, my feet heavy, my heart weighed down with unanswered questions. What was the boy's connection to us? What was the source of the strange sounds from Gregor's room? The silence in the house was suffocating. I couldn't shake the feeling that something terrible was waiting out of sight, something I couldn't stop.

That night, I lay awake, staring at the cracks in the ceiling, my mind replaying the day's events like a broken record: the boy's hesitant steps. This music had briefly filled the house, the rustling sounds from Gregor's room. None of it made sense, yet it felt connected to a larger story—a story of despair and resilience, isolation and hope, a story I couldn't understand.

The violin sat by my bed, its strings catching the faint moonlight. I thought about smashing it momentarily, severing the last tie to a life I could no longer reach. But I couldn't bring myself to do it. The violin was the last piece of me, the only thing that still felt familiar. It was mine.

I reassured myself that I would not give up. Tomorrow, I will bring Gregor another tray. I would continue to play my music. I would keep moving forward, one step at a time. It was all I could do. Even as the silence threatened to engulf me, I would not succumb. I would keep fighting, my spirit unbroken.

For now, I clung to the hope that it would be enough. And if not now, then someday, when the silence had been shattered, I would remember how to speak again. I held onto this belief, a beacon of light in the darkness of our current situation.

# 4

## Echoes in the Hallway

The morning arrived wrapped in an unsettling quiet, a stillness that settled deep in my bones and refused to let go. The house felt heavier today as if the walls were holding their breath, waiting for something—though I couldn't say for what. Gregor's door remained locked, a silent sentinel keeping us all at a distance. The hallway outside his room had turned into a forbidden space, filled with the weight of unanswered questions and an unshakable sense of dread. We were all alone in our thoughts, isolated by Gregor's silence.

With a tray of food in my hands, I stood before his door, the faint steam from the broth drifting upward. The bread was still warm, though I knew it would likely remain untouched. I had prepared it carefully this time, folding the napkin neatly and arranging everything as if organizing the tray could somehow bridge the growing chasm between us.

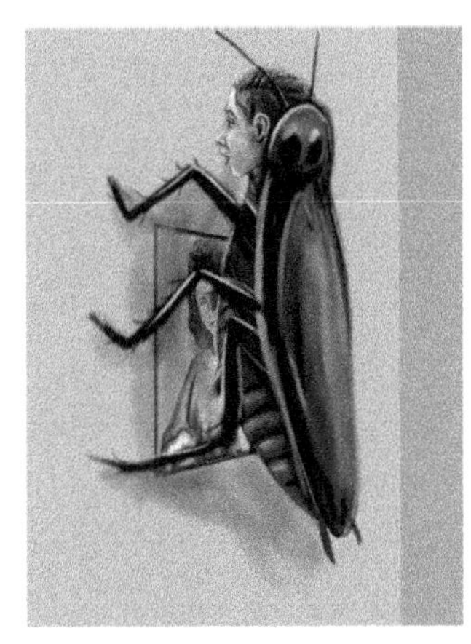

"Gregor," I called softly, my voice trembling. "It's me, Grete. Please... please say something."

The silence that followed was deafening. Not even the faint rustle from the night before, the faintest hint of life, dared to break through. It felt like the air in the house had solidified, becoming a barrier that held us apart.

I set the tray down gently, the clink of the bowl against the porcelain louder than I intended. The sound made me flinch as though I had disturbed something fragile, something that couldn't bear to be touched. I stood there momentarily, my hand resting lightly on the door, hoping for—no, willing—a response. But there was nothing—only the oppressive stillness.

"Still no word?" Father's gruff voice startled me. I saw him standing at the end of the hallway, arms crossed tightly over his chest. His expression was a mixture of frustration and something more profound—something I couldn't quite place. It was there in the tightening of his jaw, the tension in his shoulders, a sharpness that cut through the air.

I shook my head, unable to find the right words. The disappointment on his face felt like a reproach, though I couldn't tell if it was aimed at Gregor or me.

"Useless," he muttered, the word hanging in the air, heavy with bitterness.

His judgment stung more than I cared to admit, but I kept quiet. What could I say? What difference would it make? The weight of Gregor's silence was dragging us all down, and I didn't have the strength to fight it. My heart ached with the burden of our family's unspoken pain. We were all helpless in the face of Gregor's silence, unable to break through to him.

Downstairs, the tension was palpable. The clatter of dishes echoed through the kitchen, sharp and loud, as if every crash of porcelain was a commentary on the state of our house. The housemaid muttered, her words loud enough to reach me.

"Unnatural, that's what it is," she said. "A grown man locking himself away like that. It makes you wonder what's going on."

Her words struck a nerve, but I swallowed the retort that rose in my throat. What could she possibly understand? How could she, when I didn't even understand it myself? She saw Gregor's silence as unnatural, a sign of something wrong. But it was a mystery, a puzzle I couldn't solve.

"Enough," Mother snapped, her voice sharper than I'd heard in months. "You're here to clean, not to gossip."

The housemaid fell silent, but her disapproval lingered like a thick, suffocating dark cloud. I wanted to defend Gregor, to tell her she was wrong. But how could I protect him when I didn't know what I was defending anymore?

The day dragged on, the silence from upstairs seeping into every corner of the house. I tried to lose myself in the familiar motions—scrubbing, cooking, folding—but it was useless. Every creak of the floorboards, every distant sound, seemed like a reminder of the door I couldn't open and the brother I couldn't reach.

By late afternoon, I found myself back in the hallway, the tray of food now cold, the bread stale, the broth long since cooled into an unappetizing lump. I lowered myself to the floor beside it, hugging my knees. The cold wood pressed against my skin, but nothing compared to the chill inside me.

"I don't know what to do anymore," I whispered, my voice barely audible in the oppressive quiet. "You've always been the strong one, Gregor. I don't know how to hold everything together without you." My words were a confession of my own weakness, a plea for him to come back and be the pillar of strength we all relied on.

The words hung in the air, unanswered. I closed my eyes, imagining Gregor's response. I could almost see the tired smile that would pull at the corners of his mouth, the same smile he gave when he carried a burden that should have been mine. He always bore more than his share, never telling us how much it cost him. But now, that burden had crushed him, and I was left trying to pick up the pieces, not even knowing where to begin.

That night, the house felt darker than usual. The faint light from the streetlamp outside cast jagged shadows across the walls, and every creak of the floorboards, every tiny sound, seemed amplified in the silence. I couldn't sleep. Instead, I paced the hallway, my bare feet cold against the wooden floor. I stopped outside Gregor's door, my hand hovering over the doorknob. I wanted to open it, see him, and fix whatever was broken. But I couldn't. The fear of what I might find on the other side kept me frozen.

"Grete?" Mother's voice broke through the silence, fragile and thin. She stood at the bottom of the stairs, pale and drawn. "Come to bed, dear. You'll make yourself sick."

I hesitated, torn between staying and following her. Finally, I nodded and turned away from the door, knowing I wouldn't find rest. How could I when the weight of everything was pressing down on me?

The following day, hushed voices woke me. Father was speaking, his tone low and sharp with anger.

"We have to do something," he said. "We can't go on like this."

"And what do you suggest?" Mother's voice was tired, laced with exhaustion. "Banging on his door? Forcing him out? He's our son."

The chill in their words sliced through me. I dressed quickly, my hands shaking as I tied my laces. What was Father planning? Was he going to force Gregor out? The thought tightened my chest.

But when I stepped into the hallway, I froze. The tray outside Gregor's door was gone.

For a moment, I couldn't breathe. My heart pounded as I stared at the space where it had been. "Gregor?" I whispered, my voice trembling, barely audible.

There was no answer, but I thought I heard a faint shuffle, a whisper of movement behind the door. It wasn't much, but enough to spark a flicker of hope deep inside me. Maybe Gregor wasn't as lost as I feared.

For the first time in days, I believed in the possibility of change. Perhaps the silence wasn't permanent. Maybe it wasn't the end. And for now, that tiny spark of hope was enough to keep me going.

# 5

## Beneath the Locked Door

The day I finally entered Gregor's room wasn't a choice; it was a decision forced upon me by the overwhelming weight of things I could no longer ignore. The door had always been a symbol, a boundary drawn in the sand. However, when Mother collapsed on the stairs, clutching her chest and gasping for air, I realized it was time to confront the unknown.

The doctor dismissed her condition as mere "stress," suggesting it could be remedied with a few quiet rest days. However, we all understood the truth. Peace was an alien concept in this house; it had never been present since Gregor could hold everything together.

Mother retreated to her bedroom, pale and trembling. At the same time, Father began to pace like an animal in a cage, his every movement tight with frustration. His usual sharp, decisive nature had dulled in recent weeks, replaced by a restless energy that seemed to go nowhere. And so, it fell to me to do what I always did—hold the fragile threads of our family together. I cooked, cleaned, and attempted to stitch our unraveling home into something resembling normalcy.

But today, something had shifted within me. Perhaps it was the sight of Mother's collapse or the bitter realization that no one else would take the first step. Whatever it was, it pushed me toward the locked door of Gregor's room. I had been avoiding it for weeks, but now I couldn't any longer.

Carrying a tray with bread and broth, my hands shook—not from the weight of the food, but from a sense of foreboding that clung to me like thick fog. The door stood there, solid and unyielding, symbolizing everything we had ignored and all the secrets we had failed to see. I knocked softly, waiting for a response, but none came. The silence in that room was suffocating, yet I could swear I heard something—a faint rustle from within.

A gust of stale air hit me like a punch when I opened the door. The room was suffocating—dim, the curtains drawn tightly against the world outside— and dust coated every surface, softening the once-clear edges of Gregor's life. The air was heavy, with a musty smell that made me gag.

"Gregor?" I called, my voice barely a whisper, as though the room might retaliate if I spoke too loudly.

There was no answer. The rustling had stopped, but I took cautious steps into the room. Every movement felt unnatural, as if I were trespassing in a place I was never meant to be. Gregor's room had always been neat—almost obsessively so—but now it looked like a battlefield. Papers, clothes, and unidentifiable clutter were strewn across the floor as a storm had swept through. A deep ache settled in my chest. This was not the space I had known. This room, this chaos, reflected a person I no longer recognized.

I placed the tray on the desk, attempting to arrange the bread and broth in some semblance of order. Then something caught my eye—a pile of papers, half hidden beneath a mound of clothes. My fingers hesitated; touching his belongings and entering his private world felt wrong. Yet a gnawing curiosity took over. There was something here I needed to see, something that had been buried for too long.

I moved the clothes aside and uncovered a stack of letters, their edges yellowed and worn. They seemed out of place among the clutter, their deliberate placement making them feel like an intrusion into Gregor's world. My heart raced as I picked up the top letter. It was addressed to no one in particular; the seal was broken, the ink faint, and the paper smudged with age.

I unfolded the letter slowly, my fingers trembling. The handwriting was messy and frantic, as though Gregor had written it hastily.

"Dear Grete," it began.

My breath hitched, and I felt my pulse quicken. This wasn't a love letter or a casual note. It was something raw, something unspoken for far too long. I could barely bring myself to read further.

"I've been meaning to tell you... but how can I when the weight of this family hangs over both of us? I wish I could protect you from it, Grete, but I can barely protect myself. Sometimes, I think about walking away—leaving it all behind—but then I think of you, and I can't."

The words hit me with the force of a blow. My brother, the strong one, the pillar of our family, had been struggling. He carried his burdens silently, never complaining or asking for help. And I had been blind to it. Blind to how he had been suffocating, how the weight of our lives had been pulling him under. I reread the words, hoping they would change, but they didn't. They only deepened the pit in my stomach. This was not the brother I knew, the one who always had a smile on his face and a joke to share. He had become a shadow of his former self, and I had failed to see it.

I folded the letter carefully as if handling a fragile thing that might shatter if touched. I placed it back on the desk, my hands shaking. Guilt gnawed at me. I had been unable to see the signs. And now, I wondered: How long had Gregor been hiding this? How long had he been silently breaking apart?

As I turned to leave, something else caught my eye. A sketchbook lay on the floor, wedged between a chair and the desk, half-hidden in the mess. I went to pick it up, my heart pounding in my chest. I opened it slowly, my breath hitching. The pages were full of sketches—rough, hurried, and yet unmistakably Gregor's.

His drawings were always of the family—Mother at her sewing machine, Father slouched in his chair, and me with my violin under my chin. But these were not the faces I knew. These faces were twisted and distorted, as though Gregor had been seeing something in us that I could never have imagined. His lines were sharp and jagged, and the eyes—oh, the eyes were hollow, empty.

On the final page, there was an image of Gregor himself. His body was stretched, his features elongated and misshapen, his eyes dark pits of nothingness. The drawing was grotesque, monstrous even. I dropped the sketchbook, my hands trembling violently.

What had happened to my brother? What had he become behind that locked door? Fear and confusion gripped me, mirroring the turmoil within our family.

I stumbled out of the room, my heart racing in my chest, the weight of the letters and sketches pressing down on me like a suffocating fog. I returned to the sitting room, where Father was still pacing, his footsteps sharp against the silence.

"Did you speak to him?" he demanded, his voice harsh, impatient.

"No," I replied, my throat tight. "But... he's eating. That's something, isn't it?"

Father's eyes narrowed. "He needs to come out. This can't go on forever."

I didn't answer him. What could I say? How could I explain what I had just uncovered? The truth was, I wasn't sure any of us were prepared to face what Gregor had become. I felt utterly helpless, a feeling that seemed to permeate the air around us.

Later that night, as I lay in bed, the words from the letter continued to echo in my mind. "I wish I could protect you... but I can't."

Had Gregor written it for me to find? Or had it been a last-ditch effort to speak his truth, a confession he never meant for anyone to read? Either way, it felt like a lifeline—a fragile thread connecting the brother I had thought I lost to the one still hiding behind that locked door.

But it also felt like a warning. A warning that the brother I once knew had vanished, and in his place was something darker—something neither of us was prepared to confront.

# 6

## Shattered Reflections

The morning light streamed into the house like a faint apology, illuminating the cold emptiness settling into every corner. Gregor's room remained silent, but its presence loomed, a heavy weight we could no longer ignore.

By the time the day had unfolded, the house had become a mechanical world, its inhabitants moving through it with the precision of automatons, performing tasks with no heart behind the motions. Cleaning, cooking, washing—each act a desperate attempt to stave off the thoughts of everything unraveling. The walls were closing in, and no scrubbing could erase the tension in the air.

That evening, while preparing dinner, I overheard my parents' hushed conversation in the sitting room. Their voices were strained, thick with urgency, and the weight of something too long ignored.

"I don't know how long we can do this," Mother said, her voice trembling with a fear I hadn't heard from her in years.

"Do what?" Father's tone was clipped, a barricade between them, trying to silence the cracks beginning to show.

"This waiting," she replied. "This pretending that everything is fine when it so clearly isn't."

Father let out a bitter laugh. "And what would you have me do, Anna? Break down his door? Drag him out?"

"No," she whispered, her anger breaking through the exhaustion. "But maybe we should... consider calling someone. A doctor. Someone who can help."

"I'll not have outsiders meddling in our affairs," Father snapped immediately.

Mother's voice rose. "Don't we need help? It seems we've done a poor job of handling things on our own!"

The silence was thick, laden with accusations neither dared to voice aloud. In that moment, I felt the weight of their shared years—unsaid words, past regrets, and disappointments that had shaped us all. We had always been a family that kept our problems to ourselves, and now, it seemed, we were paying the price for our silence. Neither of them had the answers anymore.

I lingered near the doorway, caught between stepping forward and retreating into the shadows. Their honesty, raw and unfiltered, unsettled me more than I cared to admit. It reflected how far we had fallen—and I wasn't sure how we could ever piece things back together.

Later that night, after they had gone to bed, I crept into the sitting room. The faint scent of Father's cigar lingered in the air, mingling with the stale odor of worn-out furniture. The room felt like it was holding its breath, absorbing the bitterness and sorrow that had seeped into every crack. I sank into Father's chair, staring at the empty hearth. This place had once been warm, a gathering space for all of us. But now, it felt like a hollow shell devoid of life.

I reminisced about our past life, a time before our world crumbled. Father's business had failed, leaving Gregor as our sole provider. We were engulfed in our struggles, with fleeting moments of joy now a distant memory.

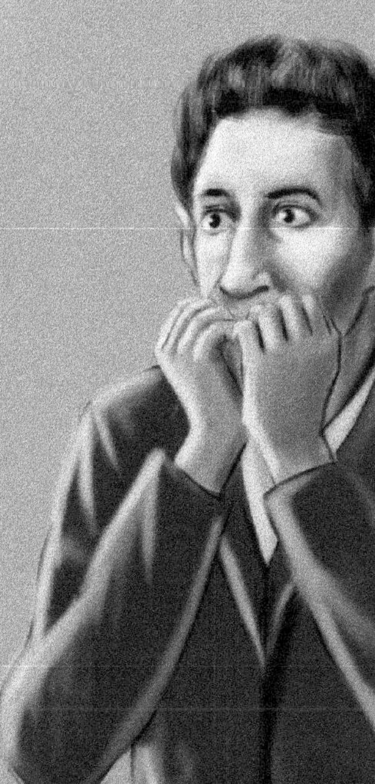

The house seemed to absorb our pain, echoing it with every creak of the floorboards and every gust of wind against the windows. It was as if the house had become a living, breathing manifestation of our suffering, offering no solace.

Father was gone the next morning before I even stirred, leaving only the remnants of his coffee and a crumpled newspaper. Mother remained in her room, claiming she was too tired to get up. I was left to carry the weight of everything left—what little remained of a family that had once felt whole.

I brought a fresh tray to Gregor's room, pausing outside his door. The air inside felt thicker now, more oppressive. I stepped in, the stifling atmosphere almost suffocating. I placed the tray carefully on his desk, avoiding the scattered papers and sketches that haunted the space.

"Gregor," I said softly, my voice trembling. "Please, just talk to me. Let me know you're okay."

There was no response. But then, a rustle—so faint, I almost missed it. My breath caught in my throat. Was it Gregor? Or was it just the wind?

"I found your letters," I whispered. "I didn't mean to, but I know now. I know how hard it's been for you."

Still, silence. A silence pressed in on me from all sides. I couldn't stand it any longer. With a heavy heart, I left quickly, shutting the door behind me as if locking away the guilt that had begun to crush me.

That afternoon, I sat at the kitchen table, staring at the untouched tray I had brought back. I had the same hope and quiet wish that he would eat and return to us this time. But nothing had changed. Gregor remained lost behind that locked door.

Through the kitchen window, I saw the boy pass by again. His movements were slower now, his shoulders heavier, burdened with an invisible weight. I longed to run outside, tell him everything, and beg his help. But what could he do? What could anyone do? The thought left me hollow, adrift in a sea of helplessness.

The silence between us was no longer just a lack of sound. It was a heavy, suffocating presence, a constant reminder of our inability to reach out to one another. The house was no longer a home—it was a prison, and we were the ones who had locked ourselves in this despair.

Then, as if to mock my thoughts, a faint knock came at the front door.

I froze. My heart raced. The boy never came this close. It couldn't be him.

When I opened the door, the housemaid stood there, arms crossed, her expression brutal and unforgiving.

"I won't clean up after him anymore," she said without preamble, her voice sharp like a blade. "Whatever's going on in that room... it's not right. And I won't have any part of it."

I blinked, stunned. "What?"

"Your brother," she said, her gaze cutting through me. "Whatever is happening in that room... it's not right. I won't clean up after it anymore."

Before I could respond, she turned on her heel and walked away, leaving me in the doorway, her words like a dagger I wasn't prepared to face.

That night, her words haunted me. Whatever was happening in Gregor's room, it wasn't normal. It wasn't something any of us could handle. But what could we do? What choice did we have but to wait?

I thought of the drawings, the letters, the image of Gregor staring back at me from the page. I thought of the crushing, suffocating silence that pressed down on this house.

This house, this family—we weren't just broken. We were hollow. And I wasn't sure if we could ever find a way to fix what had been lost.

I closed my eyes, feeling the weight of the house bearing down on me. There was no escape from it. No way out.

And perhaps, for the first time, I realized nothing might be left to save.

# 7

## The Fractured Silence

The door slammed shut so violently that it shook the house's foundation. The echo reverberated through the stillness, a loud and jarring reminder that something had finally snapped.

Father didn't even flinch. His eyes remained fixed on the paper, his fingers flipping through the pages with mechanical precision, as if the world outside could crumble and he wouldn't notice. The only sign of his emotion was the faint sneer tugging at the corners of his lips. Nothing could pierce the armor of indifference he had so carefully crafted.

Mother, however, flinched, her hands tightening around the embroidery hoop in her lap, though the thread remained untouched. Her face was drawn tight as if the absence of our housemaid was more than just the loss of help— it was the loss of something we couldn't replace, a sliver of normalcy that we could no longer hold on to. Yet, neither of us dared acknowledge it aloud.

"She was useless anyway," Father muttered, his voice flat and dismissive, as he turned another page, dismissing the gravity of it all.

I wanted to scream at him and tell him it wasn't about her usefulness. It was the truth she carried in her departure—that our family had reached a breaking point too profound to ignore. But I remained silent, the words caught in my throat, too heavy to speak.

The housemaid's absence now touched me like a weight I couldn't shake. I had become the one to fill the gap left behind, carrying the burden of a family unraveling. Mother, too weak to help, and Father, lost in his frustration, left me to scrub the floors, wash the linens, and keep the house as if it would somehow halt the decline. Every task was a mechanical act of denial, a desperate attempt to pretend everything was still as it once had been. But I bore this responsibility, this weight, with a sense of duty that was becoming increasingly heavy, threatening to crush me under its weight.

But it wasn't. I moved through the house like a specter, avoiding the sitting room where Father grumbled under his breath and the stairs where Mother sighed, buried under the weight of her despair. And Gregor, of course, remained locked away, a silent figure behind a closed door. His presence had become a hollow echo, filling the house with a suffocating silence that grew louder daily.

That evening, after preparing another meal that no one touched, I retreated to my room, longing for a moment of solitude. The violin sat abandoned in the corner, its strings now silent and uninviting. The music that once filled me with joy now felt like a betrayal, a reminder of a life that had vanished without a trace, leaving me with a profound sense of loss and betrayal.

Instead, I sat on the edge of my bed, staring at my hands, roughened and dirty, despite my best efforts. I thought of Gregor's letters, the anguish in his words, and the haunting image I'd seen in his sketchbook. This figure seemed to bend and distort, unrecognizable. The weight of our family's crisis bore down on me, a heavy burden that I struggled to carry.

How had we come to this? How had a family, once full of hope, dreams, and promise, become a shadow of itself?

The answer arrived late that night when the fight began. Their voices rose, bitter and sharp, cutting through the stillness like blades.

"You think I don't know what you've done?" Mother's voice cracked, raw with hurt and anger.

"Done?" Father's response was louder and defensive, as if to shield himself from her accusations. "What are you accusing me of now?"

"I've seen the ledgers," she spat. "The debts you're still hiding. All those nights at the café... were you even looking for work?"

Father's voice dropped into a low growl, the sound of a man backed into a corner. "Don't lecture me, Anna. You're the one who spends your days lying in bed, useless as a sack of potatoes."

The crash of something—maybe a chair—reverberated through the house, jolting me from my thoughts. My pulse quickened, and I felt the tremor of their argument in my chest as though the walls were buckling under the weight of their anger.

"Enough!" I shouted, the words tumbling out, breaking through the suffocating silence. I jumped, shaking with adrenaline, and rushed into the hallway, my frustration boiling over and filling the space with its intensity. The need for resolution, for an end to this unbearable situation, was palpable in my voice.

The noise died instantly. Father and Mother both turned toward me, their faces a mixture of shock and confusion.

"What are you doing?" I demanded, my voice shaky but firm. "Do you think shouting at each other will fix anything?"

Mother's lips quivered, and Father's face turned beet-red, his fists clenched. But neither of them spoke. I could feel the years of resentment, of unspoken words, filling the space between us.

"This family is falling apart," I said, the words bursting from my mouth before I could stop them. "And you're both too busy blaming each other to see it."

For a moment, everything stood still. The air was thick with the weight of what had been left unsaid for far too long.

Then Father spoke, his voice dripping with venom. "Maybe it's time your brother stopped hiding and faced his responsibilities."

My chest constricted with the force of his words. "And maybe it's time you started acting like a father instead of a bitter old man."

The words hit the air like a slap, reverberating between us. I hadn't meant to say them, but they spilled out in a rush, and once they were out, I couldn't take them back.

Father's face turned a deep shade of crimson. He clenched his fists, his body trembling with rage. "Watch your mouth, girl," he growled.

"No," I said, stepping back. "I'm done watching my mouth. I'm done pretending everything's fine when it's not."

Mother reached out to me, her voice softening, but I pulled away. "Grete, please—"

"No," I interrupted. "You both need to wake up. Gregor isn't coming out of that room, and this family is falling apart."

I stormed back to my room, slamming the door behind me with such force that I could feel the house shudder in protest. My pulse thudded in my ears, the weight of my anger too much to contain. The floodgates had opened, and I couldn't stop the torrent of emotions that followed.

Tears came then, hot and furious, as I sank onto the bed. I had tried to hold this family together for so long, but the cracks had grown too wide, and the weight had become too much for me to carry.

The next day, the house was enveloped in an unsettling silence. Mother remained sequestered in her room, a palpable barrier between us. At the same time, Father sat in his chair, his gaze fixed on the outside world, his eyes void of expression. I moved through the house hushedly, going through the motions of breakfast and cleaning, but the air was heavy with a sense of emptiness.

My hands shook when I took Gregor's breakfast tray to his room. I knocked softly on his door.

"Gregor?" I called out, my voice barely audible, fragile, and filled with uncertainty. "Please, just talk to me." The silence that followed was deafening, but then I heard a faint, deliberate sound like something heavy being dragged across the floor. It sent a shiver down my spine.

There was no response, but then I heard the faint scraping sound of something heavy dragging across the floor, too quiet to be accidental. My breath caught in my throat.

I opened the door slowly, my heart pounding. The room was unchanged—disarray, decay—but something felt different. Shadows flickered in the corner of my eyes, too quick to identify but enough to send a chill up my spine.

I froze. My heart raced, the sensation of being watched creeping over me like a cold breeze.

"Gregor?" I whispered, my voice trembling.

The shadow didn't move again, but the sensation lingered. I backed out of the room quickly, shutting the door behind me with a sense of finality. I couldn't stay there any longer, not with that feeling pressing down on me.

That night, as I lay in bed, the events of the day—the argument, the silence, and the shadow in Gregor's room—swirled in my mind. Our family wasn't just unraveling; it was crumbling, dissolving, piece by piece, until nothing was left but empty shells and memories of what it once was. Our collective suffering was palpable, a heavy burden we all carried.

And I wasn't sure there was anything I could do to stop it.

# 8

## The Last Note
## of Silence

The house had become unbearably still, as if the walls were holding their breath, waiting for something that never arrived. The air was thick with unspoken words and the weight of unresolved grievances. Each passing second felt like a struggle against the suffocating silence. Father's silences, which had once been merely irritating, now cut deeper and sharper with each day, like a blade. His gaze was like a knife that didn't need words to wound. Even the house seemed to groan as if it could feel the weight of everything we'd kept hidden from each other for so long. Fear and uncertainty dominated the atmosphere, casting a shadow over our every move.

And then there was Gregor.

His absence, if it could still be called that, was like a shadow behind a locked door, haunting every corner of the house. Every tray I carried back untouched, every faint noise I thought I heard from his room, every flicker of movement I caught out of the corner of my eye—it all built up, layer by layer, until the tension felt so thick I could almost taste it. It wasn't just Gregor's silence that haunted me—it was the absence of the brother I had known. I was suffocating under the weight of that absence, and no one seemed to notice, or worse, no one seemed to care. The sense of loneliness was overwhelming, a heavy cloak I couldn't shake off.

That evening, after another grueling day of cleaning, cooking, and pretending that our daily life was every day, my eyes fell on the violin in the corner of my room. It had been collecting dust for weeks, neglected just like I had been. Music had once been my escape, my solace, but now it felt like a luxury I couldn't afford, a reminder of everything we'd lost.

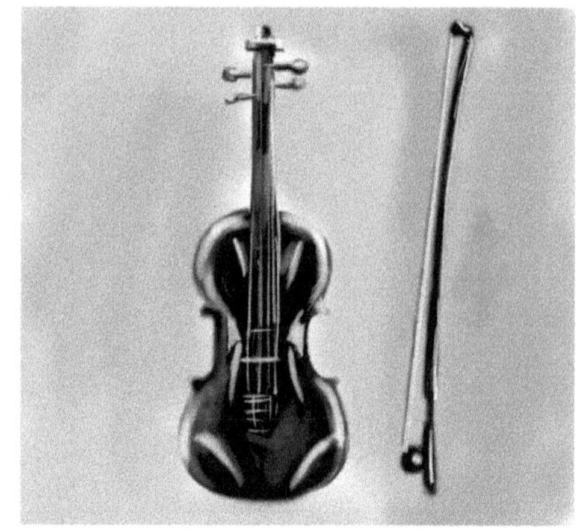

Yet, tonight, something inside me stirred. A quiet, persistent pull, urging me to pick it up. Not for Gregor, not for my parents, but for me. Just for me.

I hesitated, fingers trembling as I lifted the violin to my shoulder. The bow wavered in my grip, unsure, like a first step into the unknown. The first note was soft, tentative—like a whisper from the past. But as the sound grew, so did my resolve. The music poured from me—raw, unfiltered, unrestrained. It felt like the violin had been waiting to release what I could no longer keep inside. The weight of everything lifted for a few precious minutes, and I was free.

The music swirled around me, carrying me far above the suffocating silence of the house. It wasn't perfect, but it was mine. And in those fleeting moments, I was Grete again—the girl who once believed in music, hope, and the future.

But then, as if to remind me of everything I couldn't escape, the noise from Gregor's room shattered the fragile peace. The music was abruptly cut off, like a knife through the air. I was jolted back to the harsh reality of our family's situation.

It began as a faint scrape, followed by a rustle—something heavy being dragged across the floor. My bow faltered, the music stalling in midair. My heart raced, my body frozen in fear. I set the violin down slowly, the sense of peace evaporating as quickly as it had come.

"Gregor?" I called, my voice barely above a whisper as if the house itself might hear me. But there was no reply, only the unnerving sound that continued, growing louder and more deliberate. I stepped toward the door, each movement slow and cautious, as if not wanting to disturb the air between us.

"Please," I whispered, my voice trembling. "Talk to me."

The noise stopped abruptly, replaced by a crushing silence. I stood there, breath caught in my throat, waiting for anything—anything at all. Then, I thought I heard something else from the depths of the quiet—a faint tapping, like claws scraping across the floor. Panic surged through me, and I stumbled back, my heart pounding, as I stepped away from the door.

"What's going on?" Father's voice cut through the stillness, sharp and accusing.

I turned to see him at the bottom of the stairs, his face dark with anger, his eyes locked onto mine. My heart raced, and I felt fear creeping up my spine. "I was playing," I said, my voice shaking. "I thought... I thought it might help."

"Help?" His tone was harsh, dismissive. He climbed the stairs slowly, each step echoing his frustration. "Do you think your little concert is going to fix everything? Do you think it will make him come out?"

His words were a slap, the scorn in his voice slicing through me. I felt a fire rising in my chest. "At least I'm trying," I snapped. "What have you done? Sat in your chair, barking orders?"

Father's face flushed with rage, and for a moment, I thought he might strike me. But instead, he turned toward Gregor's door and pounded his fist against it, the force making the walls tremble. The sound reverberated through the house, a physical manifestation of his anger.

"Enough!" he roared. "You've hidden long enough. Come out and face your family!"

"Stop it!" I yelled, rushing forward to grab his arm. "You're making it worse!"

He shrugged me off, his expression twisted with years of bitterness. "He's not a child, Grete. He needs to face reality."

"Reality?" I shot back, tears streaming down my face. "The reality where you've left him to carry all your burdens? The one where you've turned this house into a prison?"

Father didn't look at me; his eyes were fixed on the door, a silent rage building behind them. His anger wasn't for me—it was for the past, for everything we had become. The silence that followed felt like the heaviest thing I'd ever carried.

"You don't understand," he muttered, his voice quieter but still bitter. "You're just a child."

"No," I said, my voice firm despite the tears. "I'm not. I've had to grow up faster than you care to admit."

The words hung in the air, unchallenged, before Father turned and walked away, leaving me standing alone in the hallway.

That night, I couldn't sleep. The argument echoed in my mind, each word cutting deeper than the last. The weight of everything—the house, Gregor, my parents—pressed down on me, suffocating me. I stared at the ceiling, the plaster's cracks mirroring our family's fractures. The violin's melody, which I had played earlier, lingered in my mind—bittersweet, haunting.

The following day, I found the tray outside Gregor's door, still untouched. The food was cold, a stark rejection. Turning to carry it back to the kitchen, I saw my reflection in the hallway mirror. The girl staring back at me was a stranger—her hair unkempt, her eyes hollow, her shoulders heavy with the burden of a family she couldn't hold together. The weight of our family's struggles was a heavy burden I couldn't shake off.

That night, I picked up the violin again—not for Gregor, not for my parents, but for myself. It was a small act of defiance, a declaration of my determination not to be crushed by the weight of our family's struggles.

Because if I didn't, I wasn't sure how I would survive.

Tomorrow, I will not give up. I will try again for myself. I will continue to fight, to hold on to the fragments of our life, and to piece them back together.

For me.

# 9

## A Life in Fragments

The silence in the house was suffocating, thick like smoke that settled in every corner and choked the air we breathed. It wasn't a peaceful quiet; it was the kind that builds a wall around you—sharp, unyielding, and heavy with the weight of things left unsaid. Every sound seemed amplified, from the scrape of my shoes on the floor to the distant hum of the outside world, which felt miles away. The walls that had once kept us safe now felt like a trap, closing in tighter with every passing hour. I felt isolated, trapped in a world of our family's struggles.

Gregor's door remained locked. On the kitchen counter, yesterday's tray sat untouched, the food cold and lifeless, just like the hopes I kept trying to hold on to. Mother hadn't left her room, murmuring about feeling unwell. At the same time, Father was gone—likely escaping to the café to bury his bitterness in coffee we couldn't afford. The rhythm of our

days had turned into something mechanical, not comforting, but burdened by an unshakable certainty that things would never change.

How much longer could this last?

I scrubbed the floors, wiped down the tables, and dusted the surfaces, trying to make the house look clean as if that would somehow clean the wounds in our lives. The dust was easier to remove than the cracks that ran deep through our family; the shadows clung to every room like a reminder of everything that had gone wrong. I was trying to cleanse the intangible, the invisible weight of our brokenness, but it never left. I felt the weight of our family's struggles on my shoulders, a burden I couldn't shake off.

As I wiped the mantle, my eyes lingered on the family portrait. It was a photograph from years ago when Gregor and I were still children before everything became fractured. Father stood proud, his hand resting on Mother's shoulder as if holding her up. Gregor and I were in front, smiling, the innocence of youth captured forever. The faces in the photograph were strangers to me now, ghosts from a life that no longer existed.

I barely recognized myself in that girl, so full of light, nor did I realize the man Gregor had become behind his locked door. Where had that family gone? The one that used to laugh, that used to dream? The past felt like a foreign land, distant and unreachable. With a heavy heart, I returned the photograph to its place, not wanting to linger on the memories that only made my sorrow deeper.

That evening, I approached Gregor's door with a fresh food tray. My footsteps felt heavier. The air around me was thick with fear and unspoken words. I placed the tray down and stood there, hand hovering over the doorknob, afraid of what I might find.

"Gregor," I whispered, trying to keep the tremble out of my voice. "Please eat. Please talk to me."

No response. Just the same oppressive silence. My hand lingered on the door for a moment before I heard it—the faint scraping sound from inside the room. It was deliberate, heavier than anything I had heard before. My heart skipped a beat, and I froze, every muscle tense with fear.

I wanted to open the door. I wanted to see Gregor, to make him face me, but a wave of dread stopped me. What if I saw something I couldn't unsee? What if Gregor was no longer the brother I remembered but something else entirely?

I turned away, leaving the tray untouched, the cold silence swallowing me whole. I couldn't keep chasing Gregor, couldn't keep knocking on a door that wouldn't open.

Later that night, as I lay in bed, memories began to flood back to me, uninvited and painful. They were fragments of a past that felt more like a dream than reality.

I remember Gregor teaching me to ride a bicycle when I was eight. His laughter was pure and carefree as I wobbled down the street. His hands steadying me, his voice full of encouragement, had been my light. It had been so easy to love him then and trust in his strength and protection.

I remembered the first time I played my violin for him. My hands were trembling, but his applause was loud and sincere. He had been so proud of me that day, and for the first time, I felt seen and understood. My music had mattered because Gregor believed in it.

And then, I remembered the letter. The raw, painful words Gregor had written:

"I wish I could protect you from it, Grete, but I can barely protect myself."

Tears slipped down my cheeks as the realization hit me like a thunderclap.

Gregor had always carried so much for us, shielding us from the worst. But I had been blind to his struggles, so wrapped up in my grief that I hadn't seen how he was slowly breaking under the weight.

The following day, I stood by the window, staring at the boy who had passed our house many times before. This time, he didn't stop. His head was down, his steps quick, as though he was trying to escape whatever had once caught his attention in our house.

I turned away, my chest tight. I had convinced myself that Gregor's fleeting glances were a lifeline, a sign that the world outside still existed. But now, even that fragile connection was gone. It felt like one more piece of the life I had clung to was slipping away.

The weight of everything pressed down on me as I tried to move through the day. My hands shook as I reached for the violin. It had been weeks since I last played, but the pull was irresistible. I lifted it against my shoulder and began to play.

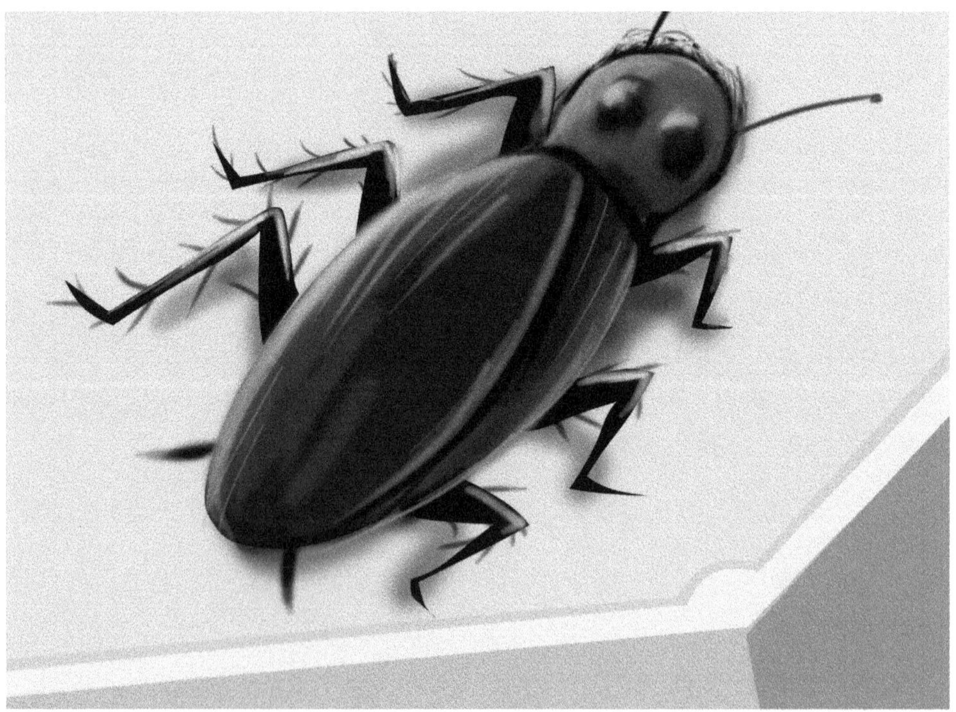

The first notes were unsure, trembling, and raw. But soon, the music began to flow—wild and uncontrolled, each note a cry, a release of everything I had kept locked inside—anger, pain, longing. The music surged through me, crashing against the silence, drowning it out, if only for a moment.

For those few minutes, I felt whole again. The music reminded me of who I had been before everything fractured. It wasn't just an escape—it was a thread, a lifeline to the girl I used to be, to the life I still longed for.

Then came the crash.

A sudden, sharp noise from Gregor's room shattered the moment. Something heavy had fallen, and my heart leaped in my chest.

"Gregor?" I called, my voice trembling. There was no answer. Only the suffocating silence that followed.

I set the violin down and rushed to the door, pressing my ear against the wood. "Gregor, are you all right?" I called louder this time, but there was still nothing.

The silence stretched deeper and darker. It wasn't the usual stillness I had expected—it was filled with an unspoken finality, an unshakable weight. I backed away from the door, my hands shaking, the fear tightening around my chest like a vice.

That night, as I lay in bed, I couldn't stop thinking about the crash, the deep silence that followed, and the broken fragments of our family scattered like shards of glass. Each of us, Gregor, Father, Mother, and me, was broken in our way, retreating into our world of pain and isolation. The weight of our collective loss was palpable, a heavy shroud that enveloped us all.

But even in the darkest moments, I couldn't give up. Not yet. I clung to a flicker of hope, believing we could piece ourselves together. Despite the fractures, we could find a way to become something more than the sum of our broken parts.

Because deep down, I still believed we could piece ourselves back together.

Despite the fractures, we could find a way to become something more than the sum of our broken parts. But as I closed my eyes, a nagging thought tugged at me:

Time was running out. And I wasn't sure there was enough left to fix what had been shattered.

# 10

## Through the Shattered Glass

The day began with a crack—sharp and sudden, like a scream breaking the silence. I awoke with a start, my heart racing. At first, I thought it was just a nightmare, a mind trick. But no, the sound lingered, jagged and unnerving, cutting through the thick silence that had swallowed our home for far too long. I threw on a shawl and stepped cautiously into the hallway, the weight of something heavy pressing down on me.

Father stood frozen at the end of the corridor, his face a storm of fury. At his feet lay the wreckage of a mirror, its jagged shards catching the weak morning light like shards of a broken soul. Once elegant, the gilded frame hung limply in his grasp as though it had also lost its will to stand.

"What are you doing?" My voice trembled, but there was a sharpness, a demand to pierce the thick air between us.

Father's eyes shot to me, wild and unfocused. "I can't take it anymore!" he spat, his voice a raw rasp, each word clawing out of him. His finger shot toward Gregor's door. "That room, that silence—it's suffocating. It's unnatural!" His desperation was palpable, a cry for help in a world of silence.

I was drawn to the door, a heavy, unseen force pulling at me. It was more than just a room—it had transformed into a symbol, a prison of unspoken truths. The weight of it bore down on my chest, a physical manifestation of the emotional burden I carried.

"Breaking things won't help," I said, though my words felt like a weak attempt at something I no longer believed.

Father's grip on the frame tightened, his knuckles pale and trembling. For a moment, I thought he might throw it at the door—smash it all to pieces, as if destroying the reflection in the glass could somehow shatter the growing distance between us. But instead, he dropped the frame with a dull thud. The sound echoed in the hallway, hollow and final, as if a clock had just ticked its last second.

The silence that followed was not peaceful—it was thick and suffocating, the kind that clings to you like a storm cloud, pressing on every breath. It amplified the emotional distance between us, a void that seemed impossible to bridge.

The rest of the day unfolded in disjointed moments, jagged and fragmented.

Mother stayed in her room, the faint sound of her sobs muffled behind the door. They were not the kind of sobs that come from raw grief but from someone who has cried themselves dry, someone whose pain has become too deep to voice anymore. Her silent suffering was a testament to the depth of her pain.

Father retreated to his chair, staring into space, his hands twitching as if he could still feel the shards of the mirror embedded in his palms.

And me? I cleaned up the glass. I picked them up one shard at a time, their sharp edges biting into my gloves. Each piece caught the light, and in the fractured reflections, I saw versions of myself—distorted, blurry, unrecognizable.

The more I stared, the more I realized I no longer knew who I was. The girl who played violin for hours, who dreamed of stages and music, felt like a stranger. The woman I was becoming—lost in the dark rooms of this house, crumbling under the weight of it all—seemed trapped, her own reflection fractured and slipping through her fingers.

That evening, I went to Gregor's door with another food tray. My steps were slower than usual, as though the floorboards resented me. As always, I set the tray down carefully and called softly, "Gregor? It's me, Grete."

For weeks, I had carried on this ritual—leaving food at his door, picking it up hours later, untouched. But tonight, something was different. As I turned to go, I heard a faint creak, the sound of movement behind the door.

I froze, my heart hammering. "Gregor?" I whispered, leaning closer.

The creak stopped, and the silence returned.

I stood there, my hand hovering over the handle, but I couldn't turn it. I wanted to see Gregor, force him to speak, and prove he was still there. But the thought of what I might find, of what he had become, rooted me in place. I backed away, leaving the tray untouched.

At dinner, the tension that had been building for weeks finally exploded.

Father slammed his fist on the table, making the dishes rattle. "He's not our son anymore," he growled, his voice thick with fury. "Whatever is in that room—it's not Gregor."

"Don't say that!" Mother cried, her face pale, her tears a silent plea. "He's still our boy. He's just... unwell."

"Unwell?" Father barked, a bitter laugh escaping his lips. "This isn't an illness. It's madness! And we've all been dragged into it."

The words struck like a blow to my chest, a hard knot of pain that wouldn't loosen. "You don't know that," I said, my voice quieter than I wanted but firm.

Father turned on me, his gaze sharp, cutting. "And what do you know, Grete?" he sneered. "You've been babying him, playing your little violin, pretending everything will fix itself if you just leave him food and wait for a miracle."

The sting of his words hit deeper than I expected, but I refused to let him see it. "At least I'm trying," I retorted, my voice rising. "What have you done? Yelled at him? Broken things? Pretended he doesn't exist?"

Father's face turned crimson. His fists clenched. The room pulsed with a tension so thick it could suffocate us all.

"Enough!" Mother's voice broke through, trembling but resolute. "This isn't helping. None of this is helping."

Her words hung in the air, fragile, like a last breath, but the damage was already done. Every word, every accusation, was another crack in the delicate structure of our family. The fractures were too deep to ignore.

That night, I sat alone in the kitchen, staring at the untouched tray I had retrieved from Gregor's door. The bread was stale, the tea cold, the soup congealed—each item a cruel reminder of our failure. We couldn't reach him. We couldn't even get each other.

I picked up my violin, its strings superb beneath my fingers. Slowly, I began to play. The melody was soft at first, but soon, it became mournful, filled with everything I couldn't say. The music swelled in the kitchen, spilling into the empty spaces of the house.

When the final note faded, silence pressed down again. It was heavier than before, a weight that refused to lift.

I stared at the violin, its strings still vibrating faintly. The echoes of the melody lingered, a haunting reminder of what we had lost—not just Gregor, but each other and maybe even ourselves.

And in that silence, I understood something I had been unwilling to admit.

It wasn't just Gregor who had changed. We all had. The realization hit me like a wave, the weight of it pressing down on my shoulders.

We all had.

We had become broken reflections of the family we once were, fractured and distorted like the shards of Father's mirror. And no matter how much I wanted to piece us back together, some things couldn't be fixed.

# 11

## The Final Breath

There are moments when silence is louder than any scream. This morning, it clung to every corner of the house, its weight pressing on me like a hand over my chest. The pale light filtering through the curtains only made the stillness more oppressive, casting elongated shadows across the floor and distorting the shapes of things as if the house were reshaping itself, folding in on itself. I couldn't shake the feeling that something inevitable was coming, and my heart raced uncertainly.

I moved toward Gregor's door, the food tray in my hands heavier than it should've been. Each step felt slower, dragging through the thick fog of my exhaustion. The air was thick with something unspoken, something suffocating. I set the tray down with a soft clink and called out, faint and fragile, "Gregor, it's me, Grete." But the room behind the door held only silence in response—an absence that spoke louder than any words could. The uneaten food, the unwashed clothes, the unmade bed! These were the daily reminders of our new reality, a reality we couldn't escape.

No reply came. Not even the faintest sound.

Weeks had passed without a single word from Gregor, and I knew deep down what that meant. The hope I once held that he might return—might wake up and be the brother I had known—had long since crumbled. There was only emptiness now, a void stretching between us like a chasm.

I left the tray, each movement mechanical, my heart weighed down by the knowledge of how much had changed. Nothing would ever be the same again.

Father returned from the café later that day. His expression was grim and closed off as he walked through the door, his eyes barely meeting mine or Mother's. She sat in her chair by the window, her hands tightly clutching a handkerchief, her gaze fixed outside, looking for something that wasn't there—something to fill the hollow space that had grown between us. We were all alone in our grief, isolated from each other by the weight of our loss.

I could see how much they had both aged. Father's once-commanding presence was now hunched, his shoulders rounded as though carrying an unseen burden that had weighed him down for years. His face had deepened, etched with lines of anger, regret, and guilt that never left him. Mother looked as fragile as a flower ready to wilt, her skin nearly translucent, veins running beneath it like delicate threads. The grief she had carried had worn her thin, hollowing her out from the inside.

I glanced at my reflection in the glass, seeing a stranger staring back. The girl who had once dreamed of performing in concert halls, of holding a violin in front of a captivated audience, felt so far away. Now, I was tied to this house, to the life we had built around the fragile hope that Gregor would return to us, that he would one day be the man he had been. That hope was gone now. I had become a shadow of the person I had once been, worn thin by the crushing weight of these walls.

Then, that evening, the quiet broke.

Father sat stiffly in his chair, his hands gripping the armrests so tightly his knuckles were white, his eyes clouded with frustration. Mother stood behind him, her hands trembling, clutching at her apron as if it were her only anchor. The tension in the room was thick, drawn taut like the strings of an instrument about to snap.

"He's not eating," Father's voice was flat but with an edge. "The trays came back untouched. He hasn't moved."

Mother's sob tore through the silence, raw and guttural, her body shaking with the force of it. "We can't keep going like this," Father continued, his voice steady but resolute. "Whatever's in that room—it's not Gregor anymore."

"No!" Mother cried out, her voice rising, desperate. "Don't say that! He's still our boy. He's just... unwell. He needs us."

Her words faltered and dissolved in the air. I could see the cracks forming, the facade of hope falling away. The truth was too hard to face, too impossible to accept. Gregor wasn't coming back.

Father stood, his movements slow, deliberate, as though the weight of the decision had already settled on his shoulders. "I'll end this," he said, his voice thick with finality. "For all of us."

The words hit me like a cold slap, and my stomach twisted into a painful knot. I watched Father move toward the door with steady steps. Mother followed, her sobs muffled behind her handkerchief. I trailed behind them, my legs heavy, my heart thudding painfully. We were all walking toward something we couldn't change, something we were too powerless to stop.

Father knocked once, then twice, before pushing the door open. The room inside was dark, suffocating with the scent of rot and decay. The air hung thick, almost tangible, like a heavy fog that pressed against my skin. I stood frozen in the doorway, struggling to adjust to the dim light.

At first, I didn't see him. The room seemed empty, the bed unmade, the sheets twisted and damp. But then, I saw it—a dark, unmoving shape hunched in the corner. It was Gregor—or what had been Gregor. His once vibrant eyes were dull and lifeless, his once agile body now a mere shell of its former self. The sight of him was a stark reminder of the cruel reality we were living in.

His body was still, shriveled, and grotesque, an alien form that didn't seem to belong in this world. He didn't move, didn't acknowledge us. His eyes were shut, his face pale and drawn. He looked smaller, as though the weight of his isolation had crushed him into something unrecognizable.

"Gregor," I whispered, the name barely a breath between my lips. It felt like a prayer, a plea, but the silence that answered me was the only response.

My father stepped forward, his face a mask of unreadable emotions, his body rigid with the moment's weight. Mother clung to the doorframe, her sobs now silent, her body shaking in shock. I forced myself to move, each step a struggle, my heart pounding. Every movement felt like dragging a weight behind me as if the truth of the moment was too heavy to bear.

And then I knew. Gregor was gone.

The days that followed blurred into one another. The house seemed emptier than ever, the silence stretching like a void. Father spoke little, his gaze distant, lost somewhere I couldn't reach. Mother's grief spilled out in waves of sobbing that filled the space between us. There were no words left. No hope. I felt like a lost soul in a world suddenly turned alien, struggling to find my place in this new reality and accept the irrevocable loss.

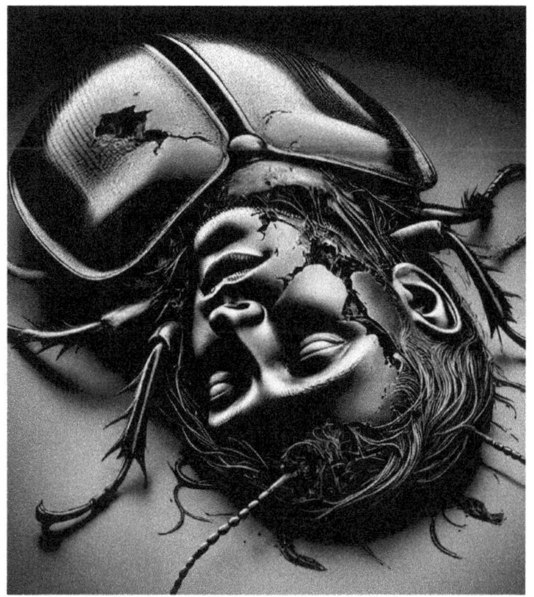

We buried Gregor quietly, just the three of us. There were no visitors, no ceremony. The cold morning light and the dirt falling in heavy clumps as we laid him to rest. Each shovelful of earth landed with a dull thud, a finality that echoed in my chest. It wasn't just Gregor we buried—it was everything he had been. His sacrifice. His love. The last thread that once bound us is now buried beneath the soil, a part of us forever lost.

I sat by the window that afternoon, staring at the street below. The boy passed by, his steps slow and measured, but he didn't glance up. I had once imagined that a passing gaze would connect me to the world outside, a reminder that life continued, even as everything within these walls fell apart. But now, even that small comfort felt distant.

I turned away from the window, my eyes meeting my reflection in the glass. The face staring back was pale and drawn. Still, there was something else there—something that hadn't been there before—a flicker of something more substantial—a quiet spark that refused to fade, no matter how much it had been buried.

I stood and walked toward my violin. The strings felt unfamiliar under my fingers, but I began to play anyway. At first, the sound was soft and mournful, a lament for what we had lost. But as the melody continued, the notes began to shift. They began to brighten, slow and uncertain but gradually gaining strength. They became something more, something hopeful. Like a gentle hand on my shoulder, the music reminded me of who I had once been and the dreams I had held. It reminded me that life and the future were still in shape, even in the face of loss. As the final note faded, the silence returned. But this time, it wasn't suffocating. It was peaceful.

I looked around the room at the house that had been both a prison and a home. It was time to let go—not just of Gregor, but of everything that had tied me to this place. To this family.

Because even in the quiet, life continues.

And so would I.

# 12

## The Weight of Goodbye

The house was quieter than I had ever known. Still, it wasn't the eerie stillness we had experienced in the days following Gregor's final breath. This silence was different—softer, like a pause between breaths. The air felt lighter, as if it had been relieved of a burden we couldn't identify. Yet beneath that calm was an unease—an unspoken understanding that this stillness was not peace but an anxious waiting for something we weren't sure we were ready to face.

Once alive with the tension of our unspoken fears and grief, the walls now exhaled a slow sigh. The house had shed its oppressive weight, only to reveal how empty we were inside. The past hung in the air like dust that refused to settle.

Father's voice broke through the quiet the morning after Gregor's burial, colder than the autumn air creeping in through the open window. "It needs to be done," he spoke. There was no room for softness, no hesitation. He didn't glance at Mother or me. Like any other, it was a simple declaration, a task. The words landed in the space between us, echoing in the hollow silence that now filled our home.

Mother, with her hands twisted around the ever-present handkerchief, nodded faintly. Her face was pale, as though the grief had sucked all the color from her. Her eyes, once sharp with concern, were now lost in some distant fog, unable to look at either of us for too long.

I wanted to say something, to stop this madness, to preserve what little of Gregor remained. But my throat was tight, my heart a lump of sorrow that lodged itself too deeply for words. So, I stayed silent. I didn't object.

We couldn't keep his room like this, living in the suspended state it represented. The room had become a tomb, the last relic of a life we had watched wither away. Still, even the thought of stepping inside, of dismantling what was left of Gregor's life, felt like a betrayal. I was torn between the need to move forward and the fear of losing the last physical connection to Gregor. It was a battle I wasn't sure I was ready to fight.

But we all knew we had to face it to move forward, so we began.

Without waiting for any further discussion, Father entered Gregor's room. His hands were steady as he opened the windows swiftly, dragging the furniture out one piece at a time. It wasn't just cleaning. It was erasure. His movements were fast and mechanical, as if eradicating the physical remnants of Gregor's life would somehow cleanse the air of the years of neglect and resentment. He worked in a blur, eyes set forward, shoulders rigid.

Mother stayed in the hallway, her face pale, her body as frail as a bird's wing. She peeked inside now and then, but she didn't enter. She didn't offer to help, and I couldn't tell if she was too exhausted to lift a finger or if it was simply too much to bear. The life that had once thrived between these walls was slipping away, and she was retreating with it.

And for me? I was frozen in the doorway, heart heavy with a grief that seemed to engulf us all. I watched as Father dumped everything Gregor had left behind in the center of the room: clothes, books, papers, each one a small fragment of him, a part of the person he had been before everything collapsed. The room had once been filled with the essence of Gregor—the quiet hum of his life, routines, and dreams. But now, it was nothing more than a hollow shell, a stark reminder of our collective loss.

His faint smell lingered in the air—sweat mixed with the must of the final days, a stench that clenched my chest. I hesitated for a moment, wondering if I could walk away. Let Father handle it. Let him erase what he couldn't bear to remember. But something pulled me forward. My gaze shifted to the desk in the corner, the same desk where Gregor had spent countless nights hunched over his work, his tired eyes scanning numbers that meant nothing to him but everything to the family he supported.

I couldn't leave. Not yet.

I stepped inside, each movement slow and deliberate, my hands shaking as I began sorting through the piles of Gregor's life. I folded shirts mechanically, stacked books without thinking, and set papers aside with numbness that seemed to come from somewhere deep inside me. The rhythmic motion of my hands should've felt soothing, but it didn't. Each object I touched reminded me of what we had lost, Gregor's sacrifices, and the life he had given away for our sake.

Among the books, I found one of Gregor's old notebooks. It was filled with numbers—client lists, schedules, scribbled notes in his precise handwriting. His job, which had drained and consumed him until he was a shell of himself, was recorded in those pages. I could almost see him sitting at this desk late into the night, eyes bleary, shoulders tense, desperately trying to keep us afloat and meet the expectations thrust upon him.

The weight of his sacrifice crushed me anew. Gregor had given everything to this family, had poured his soul into a job that never gave back, that had only been taken from him. And we had let him. We had let him because we didn't know how to do anything else. The enormity of our loss, of his sacrifice, was a burden we could never fully comprehend.

The weight of that realization made my heart feel like it was sinking.

By midday, the room was nearly bare. Father had removed most of the furniture, muttering about selling it. There was no mourning, no hesitation— just a cold practicality, as if getting rid of these things would erase the part of Gregor that had once belonged to us. The bed, the wardrobe, the desk—gone. The room, now stripped of its history, was unrecognizable. It was like walking into a place that had never held any life.

Only one pile remained in the corner—the drawings. Gregor's sketches of us, of his distorted vision of our family. His angry, desperate renditions of the people who had consumed him. I paused, my fingers hovering over the rough edges of the papers, unsure whether to hold onto them or let them go.

Part of me wanted to keep them, to preserve this fragment of him, but I knew deep down that Gregor wouldn't want that. He wouldn't want us to hold onto his pain, his fractured view of our family. He had given everything to protect us from the world outside, from the things we couldn't understand, and in doing so, he had lost himself.

With trembling hands, I packed the drawings away, placing them in a box to be forgotten. I closed the lid gently, a quiet farewell to the pieces of my brother that I would never truly understand.

The room was empty now, its bare walls exposed to the world, and I could hardly recognize it. It was as though it had never been Gregor's at all. The finality of the room's transformation was a stark reminder of the irrevocable changes in our lives.

Father stood in the doorway, expression unreadable. "We'll use it for storage," he said flatly, as though discussing a broken chair or an unused cupboard. There was no acknowledgment, sorrow, or memory of what had once filled this space.

Mother didn't speak. She stared at the empty room, eyes distant. She didn't protest. She didn't even look at Father. There was nothing left to say, and I knew that. In her silence, I found a strange sense of acceptance, a resignation to the changes that had befallen us.

I lingered momentarily, my gaze sweeping the room one last time. It was hard to believe that this space had once been filled with life. With Gregor. With his presence.

That evening, after the house had fallen into its hollow quiet again, I sat alone in my room. The violin rested in my lap, its weight familiar, grounding me as the rest of the world seemed to drift away.

I pondered Gregor's life and the sacrifices he had made. The vacant room urged us to progress and release our hold. In the hush of the night, I questioned whether we were capable of this transition, of letting go of the past and embracing the future.

I lifted the bow to the strings, and the first note broke the silence. It was soft and unsure, but it grew bolder and louder. It filled the room with sound, spilling through the cracks in the house. The music wasn't just a lament—it was a promise—a promise to remember and move forward.

Packing away Gregor's past didn't mean forgetting. It was a deliberate act of letting go, a necessary step in making space for something new, for something still to come. It was a bittersweet acknowledgment that life, in its relentless march, was waiting beyond the shadows.

As the last note faded into the silence, I knew this was the moment to step into the life waiting beyond the shadows. It was a moment filled with hope, a promise of a future that we could shape, a future that held the echoes of Gregor's memory.

# 13

## The Journey Beyond

The tram lurched forward, its wheels clattering against the tracks, seemingly eager to leave the city behind. The air inside was heavy with the scent of oil and rust, and the rhythmic hum of the tram filled the silence between us. Father, Mother, and I sat in quiet acceptance, each feeling like a stranger, burdened by our loss. The stillness that enveloped us had become a familiar companion—a presence we no longer resisted but accepted as the space we now shared, our emotions raw and palpable.

It wasn't the silence of comfort but of something much heavier. The silence of a family shattered, now sitting in the ruins, unsure how to rebuild. Like our lives, the tram was moving forward, but the direction was uncertain. Every mile felt like we were leaving behind something we would never be able to forget. Outside the window, the city blurred into a haze. Familiar streets faded into memories that seemed as

distant as another lifetime. Faces passed by, unaware of the quiet desperation inside the tram. How strange it was, I thought, that the world could move on. People walked by, continuing their days, while ours had ground to a halt. It felt like we were the only ones trapped in time, watching the world slip further away.

Father sat stiffly, his hands gripping his knees as though they were the only things keeping him grounded. His gaze was fixed ahead, unmoving as if the passing city had answers to questions he could not ask. He had been quieter than usual, and I could feel the weight of his silence pressing down on me. It wasn't anger or frustration—something deeper, something gnawing at him from within. And perhaps, I thought, the weight of that silence had started to suffocate us all.

After Gregor was gone, I couldn't stop the thought from taking root: Somebody's death is somebody else's life. Somebody's confinement is somebody else's freedom and new opportunities. Somebody's loss is somebody else's gain. The bitter truth twisted in my chest—Gregor's death had opened a space, not just for grief, but for change. For everyone else but him.

"This will be good for us," Father said suddenly, breaking the silence. His voice was flat, a careful attempt at reassurance, a beacon of hope in our despair. It was a chance to clear our heads and to think about the future.

Mother, her gaze still fixed on her lap, nodded faintly. The movement was so slight it barely registered. Her hands twisted a handkerchief in her lap, the fabric as fragile as the moment between us. She hadn't spoken much lately. Her silence had become a wall I couldn't break through. The woman who had once been full of warmth and strength seemed to have retreated inside herself, leaving only a shell of the person I had known.

"And what does our future look like?" I asked before I could stop myself. The question slipped out, sharp and biting, frustration cutting through the quiet like a knife. I wanted to believe Father and trust that this journey could offer us the fresh start we needed, but how could I imagine a future when the past still clung to us like a shadow we couldn't escape?

Father turned to look at me, his brow furrowing at my words. "Better," he said firmly as if the word alone could make it accurate. "Simpler. We can start over."

The tram jolted again, and I turned to look out the window. The city had given way to the open countryside, where land stretched out in quiet, untamed beauty. Fields of green and gold rippled under the wind, offering a serene contrast to the chaos we had left behind. It was peaceful, almost like a promise of a new beginning. The simplicity of it called to me. It whispered of a life unburdened by the weight of our loss, untroubled by the ghosts of what had been. The truth still hovered in the back of my mind—that even in the wide-open spaces of the countryside, we would carry our ghosts with us, a heavy burden I wasn't sure I was ready to bear.

Father spoke again, his voice steady but carrying a trace of something I couldn't quite place. "There's work for me in the countryside. Honest work. It'll be good for us."

"Will it?" I asked, my voice softer now, the frustration giving way to uncertainty. I wasn't challenging him—I couldn't see how work, however honest, could erase the cracks that ran through us. Could it fix what had been broken? Could it undo what had been done?

Father didn't answer immediately. His gaze returned to the passing landscape, his jaw tight. I didn't press him further. Instead, I glanced at Mother. Her face was still hidden behind her veil of silence. She hadn't moved, hadn't spoken. She looked adrift, her eyes darting around the tram before settling on the handkerchief she twisted in her hands once more. She was untethered from the world around her.

The tram slowed as it approached a small station, and a man boarded. He was dressed in a worn coat, his hat pulled low over his eyes. He moved to the back and sat down, his presence a quiet reminder that we weren't the only ones traveling, that everyone carried their burdens and stories. I watched him momentarily, wondering where he had come from and where he was going. Did he, too, feel the weight of the past pressing down on him? Did he also dream of new beginnings, or was he trapped, like us, in the cycles of loss and change? The thought made my chest tighten. It didn't matter how far we traveled; we would always carry our ghosts.

As the tram moved again, I turned back to the window, watching the countryside blur into a patchwork of green and gold. I let my mind wander, imagining a future that seemed just out of reach, its contours uncertain and hazy.

I imagined playing my violin again—not in isolation, but in a place filled with warmth, surrounded by people who cared. I imagined the music flowing through me, filling the air with something beautiful that could push away the darkness. I imagined laughter, lightness, and joy returning to our lives. But even as I let myself dream, the ache in my chest reminded me how fragile those dreams were and how easily they could slip through my fingers.

When the tram stopped at the station, the air felt calmer, the evening breeze brushing against my skin. The station was small, almost unnoticed, with only a few scattered leaves blowing across the platform. The scent of wildflowers and freshly turned soil filled the air, a sharp contrast to the heavy, stale atmosphere we had left behind in the city.

Father squared his shoulders, his movements deliberate as he stepped off the tram. There was no hesitation in him now, no looking back. He walked ahead as if bracing himself for what lay in the future, whatever it might be. Mother followed her grip on her handkerchief loosening, her eyes scanning the new surroundings as if searching for anything that might feel like home.

I lingered for a moment on the platform, feeling the breeze wash over me. It felt like a beginning, though I knew well that beginnings weren't always clean or easy. They were messy and full of doubt and fear. But they were necessary. Without them, there could be no moving forward.

As we walked toward the town, I felt the weight of the past with each step, its shadow never far behind. But there was something new alongside it—a faint flicker of hope. It wasn't a promise of instant healing, but it was enough to make me believe that something better might still be waiting for us.

I glanced at Father, his steps steady, and then at Mother, whose grip on the handkerchief had loosened just a little. I realized then that moving forward wasn't about forgetting the past. It was about carrying it with us, allowing it to shape who we became without letting it define us entirely. Because even in the quiet, life continued.

And so would we, with an acceptance that brought reassurance, peace, and wisdom from our experiences.

# 14

## Beyond the Glass

We returned to the station and continued our journey. The tram windows were streaked with grime, their surfaces smudged and uneven, distorting the view outside. Beyond them, the world appeared like a fragmented dream—fields of green and gold, trees shifting into unrecognizable shapes, all blending into a surreal landscape. Each passing scene felt out of reach, like a puzzle whose pieces would never fit. I found myself staring, my mind attempting to force the images into coherence as if looking long enough might piece them back together and make them whole again. But no matter how long I watched, they always eluded me.

Beside me, Mother sat with her hands folded tightly in her lap, her posture stiff and rigid, her gaze fixed on the same fragmented world outside. The sunlight streamed through the window, casting a soft, pale glow on her face. Yet, despite the warmth of the light, there was a coldness in her expression—a tension that even the sun couldn't

soften. Her silence was thick, almost palpable, and in that silence, I felt the distance between us growing wider. The woman I once knew, full of warmth and strength, had faded away, leaving only a shell behind.

"Do you think it will be different there?" she asked suddenly, her voice soft, almost afraid of the question.

Her words startled me. Mother had become a ghost of sorts in the last few weeks, barely speaking, her thoughts locked away behind a wall of silence. For her to ask a question, especially one so full of vulnerability, felt like a crack in that wall. A glimpse of the person she had once been.

"I don't know," I replied, my voice heavy with uncertainty. "I hope so."

She nodded, her eyes still fixed on the blurred countryside. Her hands gripped her handkerchief so tightly that the fabric seemed struggling to hold its shape. "I used to think... if we just waited long enough, things would return to how they were. But now..." Her voice faltered, a soft, bitter laugh escaping her lips. "Now, I know that was foolish. Nothing ever goes back to the way it was."

Her words hung in the air, heavy with the weight of truth. She was right, of course. The past was a distant echo, irretrievably lost, and no amount of waiting or wishing could bring it back. The burden of that truth settled in my chest, a stone that refused to budge. We were left with nothing but the open, uncertain future, a road we were too afraid to tread.

"What now?" I asked, the question slipping out before I could stop it. I wasn't sure if I was asking her or myself. I needed to hear something that didn't feel like an end. Something that could point us toward a way out of the darkness, a path that didn't seem so daunting.

Mother hesitated, her fingers tightening around her handkerchief. "Now we move forward," she said softly, her voice lacking the strength I had hoped to hear. "But it's hard to let go of what we've lost."

My response was silent. How could I articulate the impossibility of letting go? Leaving behind Gregor, the life we once knew, and stepping into a future overshadowed by a vivid and painful past felt like a betrayal. Yet, remaining in the suffocating place of grief was equally unbearable.

Across from us, Father sat with his arms crossed, his face unreadable. He hadn't spoken since we boarded the tram, and I could feel the weight of his silence pressing down on the space between us. His silence wasn't the same as Mother's. Hers was a fragile, vulnerable quiet. His was complex, impenetrable, a wall I could never climb. He stared out the window, his eyes distant, lost in thoughts I couldn't even begin to understand.

Our father, the unyielding pillar of our family, now seemed to be crumbling under the weight of his expectations. Once filled with determination, his eyes now held a hint of uncertainty. He was no longer the one who guided us forward but a man lost in his battles, unsure of his next step.

The tram rattled along the tracks, its wheels grinding against the metal, both soothing and maddening. The scenery outside seemed to blur and shift. For a moment, I thought I saw Gregor's face reflected in the glass—just a fleeting shadow, a shape stretched and distorted by the imperfections in the window. I blinked, and he was gone, replaced by my own reflection.

The girl looking back at me was familiar, yet strange. Her eyes were mine, her features too, but her face had changed. It was more complex now, more defined by what I had lost, shaped by grief and resilience. She looked like someone who had seen the worst of life and survived. But at what cost? Could you survive this and remain the same person you once were?

I turned away quickly, unable to meet her gaze for too long. It was easier to look at the world outside, even if it, too, felt like something I couldn't touch. The glass between us seemed to separate everything—my past, my family, my grief—from the world that kept moving forward, indifferent and unfeeling.

The tram slowed as it approached a final small station, the screech of the brakes pulling me from my thoughts. I realized I had been holding my breath, waiting for something to change.

The station was small, the platform surrounded by trees and wildflowers, a quiet place far from the city's noise. The air here was fresh and light, untouched by the suffocating heaviness of the place we had left behind. I felt like I could breathe again for the first time in weeks.

"Is this it?" Mother asked, her voice trembling slightly. It was not just a question about the destination but a fragile hope that the pain might end here.

Father stood and adjusted his coat, his movements deliberate. "This is it," he said flatly, his voice steady but lacking the conviction that used to fill him.

We gathered our things silently and stepped off the tram, our feet touching the platform as the cool air wrapped around us. The breeze carried the scent of earth, grass, and wildflowers, a sharp contrast to the musty air inside the tram. I let it wash over me for a moment, hoping it would carry away some of the weight I had been carrying.

The town stretched beyond us, unassuming and straightforward—narrow streets, modest houses. It wasn't much, but it was a beginning—a beginning that didn't promise instant relief, joy, or healing. It was simply the first step toward something new.

Walking towards the house, I saw my reflection in a shop window. The girl staring back at me was tired, but there was a glimmer of something new in her eyes—a sense of acceptance. She was not the same person she was before, and that was okay. Perhaps surviving meant embracing change and becoming someone new.

That night, in the quiet of the tiny house, I sat by the window, my violin resting in my lap. The stars overhead were faint but steady, their light distant but constant, like a reminder that the world was much larger than the small piece we inhabited.

I began to play. The music was soft at first, hesitant, but with each note, it grew stronger. The melody filled the room and spilled out into the night. It wasn't a song of sorrow—a song of quiet hope—a promise to myself that I wouldn't let the past define me, that I could move forward, even if it meant becoming someone new.

Through the glass, I saw my reflection once more. This time, the girl smiled. She wasn't who I had been, but maybe that wasn't bad. She was a version of me that had grown, embraced change, and emerged stronger.

The journey wasn't over, and the pain would never entirely leave. But for the first time, I felt like I could begin again. And that was enough.

# 15

## The Sound of Freedom

The house at the edge of town felt like a strange kind of rebirth—a new beginning forged in the quiet aftermath of devastation. Here, where the cobblestone streets met the dirt roads and the endless fields stretched beneath the sky, we began to rebuild. The house was small, with freshly painted walls, and the air still carried the scent of untouched wood and paint. Sunlight streamed through the windows, filling the rooms with an almost intrusive brightness as if the house was pushing the past aside and determined to illuminate every corner. It wasn't just a house but a symbol of our resilience and hope for a new beginning.

It wasn't much, but it was all we had left—this fragile foundation upon which we were meant to start over. For the first time in months, I felt something I hadn't dared to acknowledge: a tiny spark of hope, a beacon in the darkness of our grief.

The house's rooms were bare—only the most necessary items filled the space, leaving an unsettling and oddly comforting emptiness. The silence invited new thoughts and opportunities. The absence of clutter felt like a quiet canvas, waiting to be painted with the future.

Father, with a newfound determination, threw himself into his new job at the factory. He woke early and returned home late, his hands calloused, his face drawn. His movements were purposeful, an intensity that had been absent for so long. He wasn't just working for survival; he was working to create anything that could push us all forward. It was as if the weight of our family's survival had once again rested on his shoulders, but this time, he didn't seem to carry it alone. He took it with a fierceness, like a grown-up on a mission, with a direction that had only appeared after Gregor's death.

Mother, too, immersed herself in the daily tasks of making a home. Her hands, though delicate, moved steadily, her body still fragile but strong in its own way. The weariness that had clung to her was still there, but something softer had returned to her demeanor. A faint smile would occasionally tug at the corners of her lips, and in her presence, I could almost feel the echoes of a life full of joy before grief had stolen it. Her resilience was a testament to the strength of the human spirit in the face of adversity.

And then there was me. I turned to my violin. The instrument had been my refuge during the darkest days, its strings my lifeline to the world outside the walls of our apartment. But now, in this quiet house, it became something more. My music no longer sought to drown out the noise of pain—it sought to find clarity. It sought to break free from the weight of grief that shackled us all. What once was a lament now became a declaration. A celebration of survival, of endurance. After all, someone's loss always leaves space for someone else to breathe, dream, and live. My transformation was a testament to the indomitable resilience of the human spirit.

I wasn't playing for an audience. I wasn't playing for my family or Gregor, whose absence lingered like a ghost. I wasn't even playing for anyone but myself. Each note was a step toward something new, a way of reclaiming a part of me buried under the years of sacrifice, duty, and grief.

One morning, I stood before the small mirror in my room, the sunlight spilling through the curtains like liquid gold. The reflection that greeted me was unfamiliar—a stranger's face staring back, but not in the way I'd once thought. It wasn't a face distorted by sorrow or duty but one that seemed to hold a quiet strength. My features were sharper now, my gaze steadier. It was as though the storms I'd weathered had carved something deeper inside me— something unshakable. This was not just a physical change but a reflection of my personal growth and transformation.

I thought of Gregor—not the twisted, alien figure he had become in his final days, but the brother I once knew, the young man who had sacrificed everything for us. He had been the pillar holding us up, even as his dreams crumbled beneath the weight of responsibility. His sacrifice had been so profound, so complete, but in the end, it had been for nothing. And yet, something new was rising from the ruins of that sacrifice. We were rising. I was rising.

And that thought hit me with the force of a revelation. Gregor's story wasn't one of unrelieved despair. It was the story of sacrifice, yes, but also of transformation. In his absence, we had no choice but to change. And so, we did. I did. The loss of one life had, in the end, made space for the living.

I carried my violin outside, where the air was crisp, and the sky stretched out before me, an endless expanse of possibility. The fields seemed to stretch forever, the wind rustling through the trees, carrying the sounds of life in its wake—birds, insects, the distant hum of the earth itself. The world outside was vast, and for the first time, it didn't seem threatening. It seemed like a canvas waiting to be painted.

I played. Like birds taking flight, the notes soared from my fingertips, intertwining with the world's melodies. I wasn't playing to escape; I wasn't playing to mourn. I was playing to seize this moment and my place in the world. The music ascended, a testament to survival, liberation, and the strength that emerges when you've been shattered and then choose to reconstruct, piece by piece, note by note.

As the final note reverberated into the open air, a shift occurred within me. The burden that had weighed heavily on my chest for so long, the sorrow that had permeated every breath, began to lift. It wasn't completely gone—but it was lighter. I could breathe. For the first time in a long time, I could truly breathe.

Father spoke as we sat around the small kitchen table that evening. His voice was rough, like a man who hadn't used it in days. He had been quiet for so long, buried in the work that consumed him. But now, he spoke, his words heavy with meaning.

"You've been playing a lot," he said, his voice gruff but not unkind.

I nodded, unsure of how to respond.

"It's good," he added after a pause. "You should keep doing it. I remember when I used to play; it was my escape, too." His words carried a weight of understanding, a shared experience I hadn't realized we had.

His words, though simple, carried more weight than just an observation. They were an affirmation of me, of the person I was evolving into.

Mother, her hand resting gently on mine, smiled. "It's beautiful," she said, quiet but sincere. Her eyes held a deep understanding, a silent reassurance that I was on the right path.

It wasn't just the music they were acknowledging. It was me. Not the dutiful daughter. Not the grieving sister. But someone else—someone who had survived, had endured, was finally starting to break free. Their words weren't praise, not really. They were a recognition of a change that had been coming for so long but that I had only just begun to see.

The following day, I stood before the mirror again. The girl who looked back at me wasn't just a sister or a daughter. She had withstood loss, faced the dark, and emerged with the strength to walk into the light. I saw a glimmer of hope in her eyes, a spark of resilience I hadn't seen before. The road ahead was uncertain, but it no longer held the same weight. It no longer felt like something to fear.

I was ready to step into the unknown and claim the world that had once seemed so vast and distant.

This wasn't just the end of one story. It was the beginning of something new.

And that was enough for the first time in a long while.

*Thank you!*

**Learn more at the author's website:**
ramckhatri.com

**Read or listen to all chapters now on Substack:**
ramkhatri.substack.com

www.ingramcontent.com/pod-product-compliance
Lightning Source LLC
Chambersburg PA
CBHW040542170726
48295CB00012B/567